This book
belongs
to

Amber Michelle
2 yrs. old
x-mas
1994

Given by:

Gramma + Grandpa Kotas

The Ugly Duckling

By Hans Christian Andersen

Retold by Andrea Stacy Leach

Illustrated by Michael Hampshire

DERRYDALE BOOKS

New York / Avenel, New Jersey

It was summertime in the country. At the edge of a pond, a mother duck was waiting for her eggs to hatch. After a long time, they finally began to crack. "Peep, peep," the ducklings said.

"Quack, quack," replied their mother. "Look at the big world around you." The mother duck was delighted with her ducklings. But then she looked around. "Oh dear," she cried, "the biggest egg is still in the nest! And this egg is much darker than all the others!"

"I am sure it is a turkey egg," said another duck.

At last the large egg cracked. "He doesn't look like the others," the mother said. "I wonder if he *could* be a turkey?"

The next day the mother duck took her ducklings for their first swim. "Quack, quack!" she said. "Follow me. I'll take you to the hen yard and introduce you to the other ducks. Stay close now, and look out for the cat."

The other ducks in the hen yard did not like the big, gray duckling. They chased and bit and pushed him all day long.

"You are so ugly we wish the cat would get you," they laughed. Even his mother finally said, "You really *are* an ugly duckling."

The duckling was so unhappy that he ran away to a swamp where many wild geese lived.

"You *are* ugly, but you seem nice," the geese said. "We are going to fly south for the winter. Do you want to come with us?"

Bang! Bang! Before the duckling could answer the geese, the swamp was filled with hunters. Their dogs splashed around, looking for ducks. The geese flew away, and the ugly duckling was so frightened he hid in the grass for a long time. Finally, the hunters left, and the duckling ran away as fast as he could.

Soon the duckling found a quiet lake with other ducks, but once again they ignored him because he was so ugly.

One evening as the sun was setting, a flock of swans flew above the lake. Their feathers were snowy white, and they had long, slender necks. The ugly duckling thought that the swans were beautiful. He stretched his neck to the sky to try to get a better look at them. As he gazed up at the swans, the duckling knew he would never forget the graceful way they traveled through the sky.

The weather grew colder, and the lake turned to ice. The poor duckling was cold and hungry. One morning, a farmer found him and took him home. Inside the cozy house, the farmer's wife fed the duckling and nursed him back to health.

When the farmer's children saw the duckling was feeling better, they wanted to play with him. The youngsters pretended they were ducks, too, and ran toward him, flapping their arms. The duckling did not know the children were playing, and he was frightened. He tried to run away, but he fell into the milk pail and then into a barrel of flour. What a mess he was! The duckling shook himself off and ran outside to hide in the swamp.

The ugly duckling spent the long winter huddled in a thick patch of reeds. When he finally heard the larks begin to sing, he knew that spring had come! The duckling spread his wings. How strong and powerful they had become! The duckling began to run in the warm spring air. He flapped his wings, and suddenly he was flying.

The duckling flew high above the swamp and the farmland nearby. Beyond the barn was a lovely garden with a beautiful pond. Below him he saw the swans that he had thought were so beautiful. "I want to be near them," he said to himself. "I am so ugly they probably won't want to be friends with me, but I'd like to meet them anyway."

When the duckling landed on the water, he was not brave enough to approach the lovely birds. Instead, he settled down and gazed at the graceful swans. Then he saw that they were coming to meet him. The ugly duckling was sure that they were going to ask him to leave their home.

The poor ugly duckling bent his head shyly and waited for the swans to start squawking at him. But what was that he saw in the water? It was his own reflection, and he was no longer an ugly duckling. He was a swan! Suddenly he understood. It did not matter that he had been born in a duck's nest, because he had come from a swan's egg.

The other swans welcomed him and made him one of their family. The young swan's heart filled with joy. But as he swam off to be with his new friends, the swan made a promise to himself. "If I ever see an ugly duckling, I will be as kind to him as I always hoped others would have been to me."